COLOURS AROUND ME
Blue

Anita Loughrey

QED Publishing

What is blue?

Blue is a colour.

This is the colour blue.

Look at the picture of the picnic.

What can you see at the picnic that is blue?

Answer: The blanket is blue.

Who is going to the blue house?

Follow the paths to find out.

Elliott

Helena

Fred

Gunita

3

Finding blue

Point to the things
that are blue.

How many blue things
can you see?

Answer: 4 blue things

Matching blue

Look at the balloons.

Point to the two blue balloons.

Blast off!

Help the rocket through the maze to get to the blue planet.

How many blue stars does the rocket pass on the way?

Answer: 5 blue stars

Blue shapes

Blue things can be different shapes.

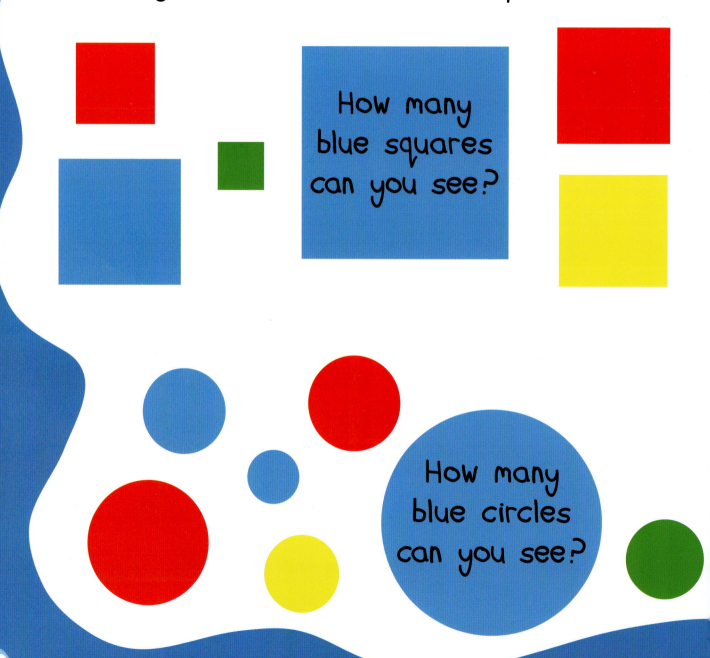

How many blue squares can you see?

How many blue circles can you see?

Answer: 2 blue squares, 3 blue circles

How many blue rectangles can you see?

How many blue triangles can you see?

What blue shapes can you see around you?

Answer: 2 blue rectangles, 3 blue triangles

Big and small

Blue things can
be different sizes.

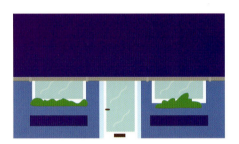

big

bigger

small

biggest

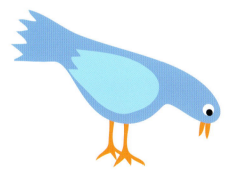

smaller

smallest

Odd ones out

Some things here
are the wrong colour.

sun

frog

dolphin

whale

raindrops

leaf

apple

umbrella

sea

sunflower

Which things should be blue?

Shades of blue

Blue can be different shades.

dark blue

blue

dark blue

light blue

blue and
light blue

light blue

What shades of blue
can you see around you?

Blue in the sea

Can you find all these blue things in the sea?

coral

shell

fish

dolphin

shark

jellyfish

octopus

Which of these blue things would you like to spot in the sea?

17

Blue is for cold

Point to all the blue
things you can see in
this ice-cold picture.

scarf

penguin

whale

water

iceberg

seal

hat

Is it cold today?
What blue things
can you see outside?

19

Blue is for the sky

Point to the blue things you can see in the sky.

aeroplane

hot-air balloon

helicopter

balloon

kite

bird

dragonfly

Look out of the window.
Does the sky look blue today?

21

Blue at bedtime

Point to the blue things you can see in the bedroom.

teddy bear

pyjamas

slippers

duvet

toy box

alarm clock

book

Have a look around your bedroom. What blue things can you see?

Notes for parents and teachers

This book has been designed to help children to recognize the colour blue and to distinguish blue from other colours. The vibrant activities make learning fun and use the environment around them to reinforce what they have learned.

• Read the instructions to the child. Allow time for the child to think about the activity. Encourage them to discuss what they see.

• Praise the child if they recognize the items in the book. If any of the items are unfamiliar, explain what they are and where they might be found.

• If possible, take the child into the environment you have talked about so that they can observe items pictured in this book. Encourage the child to spot blue objects using ideas from this book.

• Remember to keep it fun. Stop before the child gets tired or loses interest, then continue on another day. Children learn best when they are relaxed and enjoying themselves. It is best to help them to experience new concepts in small steps.

Other activities you could try:

• Play games such as 'I spy': saying "I spy with my little eye a blue thing beginning with...". If the child is not yet familiar with the alphabet, you could say the initial sound of the word rather than the letter name.

• Cut pictures from catalogues and magazines of different-coloured objects and ask the child to sort them, or match them to the pictures in this book.

• Ask the child what blue things they can see when you are outside, at home, or looking in other books.

• Experiment with colour using different media such as paint, crayons, pastels and coloured paper.

Illustrator: Sue Hendra
Editor: Lauren Taylor
Designer: Fiona Hajée
Educational consultant: Jillian Harker

Copyright © QED Publishing 2011

First published in the UK in 2011 by
QED Publishing
A Quarto Group company
226 City Road
London EC1V 2TT

www.qed-publishing.co.uk

A catalogue record for this book is available from the British Library.

ISBN 978 1 84835 535 4

Printed in China